HOW TO AVOID BREAKUP

A TORCHBEARER TO THE YOUTH

RAGHAV M S

Copyright © Raghav M S
All Rights Reserved.

This book has been published with all efforts taken to make the material error-free after the consent of the author. However, the author and the publisher do not assume and hereby disclaim any liability to any party for any loss, damage, or disruption caused by errors or omissions, whether such errors or omissions result from negligence, accident, or any other cause.

While every effort has been made to avoid any mistake or omission, this publication is being sold on the condition and understanding that neither the author nor the publishers or printers would be liable in any manner to any person by reason of any mistake or omission in this publication or for any action taken or omitted to be taken or advice rendered or accepted on the basis of this work. For any defect in printing or binding the publishers will be liable only to replace the defective copy by another copy of this work then available.

Dedicated to: All the breakup guys and girls!

Contents

Preface

I could see so many breakups in our day-to-day lives. This personal problem affects our personal lives. Our personal lives affect our professional lives. That affects our entire lives completely. I wanted to share all the knowledge and make the youth lead a happy-peaceful relationship. This book will be a mentor for couples and people in a relationship, how to treat and how not to treat in a relationship, how to resolve the misunderstanding, breakup and post-breakup life etc.

If you are reading this book, you can get to know the in and out of love, but it can't guarantee you can avoid a breakup. If you are studying Bachelor's of Philosophy, you can get a degree in philosophy but cannot become a philosopher. The same applies here. It all depends on the couple and their bond.

Join the club of "How to avoid a breakup"

Acknowledgements

Thanks to

Warning: It would be a massive vote of thanks. If you feel tiring, skip this page and directly navigate to "Synopsis"

First of all, I was determined to convert a spark into a complete non-fiction despite all odds. This is the non-fiction you are holding in your hand.

Readers- you might have spent 200+ bucks for anything to buy; instead, you choose this book. Thank you. I assure you I would keep writing such innovative stories with a simple writing style.

Publisher- Notionpress, for their free of cost publishing.

My family and friends, lecturers, relatives.

God- I loved to thank him. Not only for this novel, right from my shaky birth to present today. You cared and guided me a lot. I believe the path you showed to me. If you are advised me, I don't know how my life would have shaped.

Last but not least, thanks to ex.... **Ex**(actly) what you are **ex**(pecting) here to **ex**(hibit). As I'm not an **ex**(pert) to **ex**(clued) the vote of thanks **ex**(cluding) few people. Though I'm not an **ex**(trovert), I don't **ex**(ploit) anyone here. Enough of **ex**(panding) further and enough of **ex**(cuse), I'm **ex**(cited) to navigate to the synopsis.

Prologue

1. **Relationship Series:**

    Are you in relationship or re(e)lationship?
    Propose: how, when, where?
    How to treat her?
    Personalized gifts
    The dark side of love
    The marriage negotiations
    2. Breakup series:
    How to resolve the fight with your girlfriend?
    What if misunderstanding happens again and again
    Why does the breakup happen?
    How to handle the break-up!
    What should we do after breaking up?

Relationship series Are you in relationship or re(e)lationship?

We have all probably come across the story of the tortoise and the rabbit. The tortoise finished the race first, ahead of the rabbit, in spite of the rabbit's talent for running fast. Here, we aren't linking to this story. However, connecting the rabbit and tortoise to our love lives is a stretch. Love should be like a tortoise, not like a rabbit. **It is not how quickly we fall in love or how early we fall in love, but how closely we understand each other that sets the stage**. For love to be understood and trusted, it takes months and years. We cannot judge a person by just hanging out with a date. In fin-love terms, love should be like the Sensex: stable, predictable, and understandable; not like crypto currency: unstable, unpredictable, and volatile. In modern times, people tend to fall in love quickly and break up even quicker, in a coffee-consuming time.

Respect + Trust + Understanding + Affection = Love.

A Life Partner is a combination of the following elements: partner + therapist + motivator + life coach.

When someone says "Love," an iron rod sticks in my head with this proverb: "Rome can't be built in a day." I'm not sure whether Rome can be built in a day or so, but love can be built in a day. It is being built in on a daily basis. I believe this proverb is specifically suitable for love. Love needs time, patience, and sincerity.

Some of them fall in love quickly and break up with them quickly. We all heard what some of our friends might have said: I had "Love at first sight." Not all "love at first sight" is true or ends on a happy note. Sometimes, "love at first sight" would turn into "break at next sight".

Love is not about sharing information. **"Love" is behaving with each other.** Personally, I'm not a great fan of online love. How could you judge a person online? Through online, you can just know the person through that person's perspective. Those are just conveyed by the person. But, that's not love. You have to know the other person inside and out, without the other person telling you about themselves. You have to literally go with them, be with them, watch him/her, observe him/her, understand him/her, and then fall in love. We don't always know who we're talking to (for example, a fake profile or one of their friends may text on their behalf). Let me come up with a hands-on example, an interesting story, Imagine a "Y" boy and a "Z" girl following each other on insta, but they don't know each other personally, simply insta-friends. One fine day, "Y" started texting "Z" through insta, and they started texting like this:

"Hi. Y here. I've been following you on insta for the past 4 months. "Let me introduce myself," narrates "Y," the boy. He initiated the conversation, and he shared who he was like, what he was like, where he was, his college, and his job.

"Hi. Good to know that. "I'm working at ABC company as so and so," says "Z," the girl. Here, they both introduced each other.

"What do you like?" asks Y.

"I love reading books, browsing, and sketching," says Z. "Wbu?"

"Playing cricket, watching movies and hanging out with friends," says Y.

"I love Maddy and Khan in acting," says Z.

"I love Kapoor and Singh in acting," says Y.

So, here, Y and Z come to know each other's likes, hobbies, likes, company, work, work experience, etc. They are sharing their knowledge and, in the course of time, if they like each other, one of them will propose, the other accepts, and love blossoms. But, in reality, they met online, got to know each other online, and dated online. Will they marry online? Of course, it's impossible, even in Corona times. They got to know each other in person, and that's where the real relationship started. See, I'm not against online love or the ones who get hooked through social media. But the point is, not all that glitters is gold. Not all online dating turns into a beautiful relationship. Here, in our hands-on story, through online chatting or dating, Y and Z came to know each other through their perspective, through their own words. That's not love. The other person should tell them who he or she is. They are sharing the information. Love shouldn't be information-based. It should be experience-based. One should move and experience life with their partner to declare it as love or a relationship. Unless a person moves with another person or has experience with another person, we can't declare it as love or a relationship. "Y" should not reveal his identity here. "Z" must know who "Y" is. "Z" should move in with

"Y", "Z" should have dinner with "Y", "Z" should spend some time with "Y", and then "Z" should decide whether "Y" is the kind of person she is looking for, whether All the above statements are applicable from a male perspective as well. By the way, I don't encourage dating to know each other in person or not to love anyone online. That's not my point. My point is that by getting to know each other through physical presence, keen observation, and lively interactions, we can understand each other. Love takes time. Understanding takes time. We can choose our girlfriend or boyfriend through chats. That's the reason-classroom love and office love has been more common and happier than online love.

So, before you can love them, you must first understand them. So, before understanding, be with them. Before you fall in love, learn about their + and - signs. Love is not the money to transfer it easily through online transactions. It is that we are giving that person our heart, affection, love, time, energy, and, most importantly, our soul. So, judge that person personally before you surrender yourself.

A life partner or lover can turn you into anything. Wife and girlfriend are the world's most underappreciated motivational speakers.

Remember that love can turn a stone-hearted person into a soft-hearted person and a soft-hearted person into a stone-hearted person. There would be so many problems the partners would be facing. Mind you, there is always a solution to every problem and a problem to every solution! A common solution for the partners is to be supportive of each other.

The major problem in a relationship is being adjusted. People tend to adjust to their life partner.

Never adjust! Accept!

Even my life partner believes too much in astrology. I didn't try to change her. I let her be the way she was. I accepted her. Not adjusted. Our minds can only accept, can't adjust to it!

A fine relationship should be like a fish and water, not a fish and a fisherman!

When we first meet a person, we don't have an impression of them. In the course of time, after getting to know their real character, we develop a huge respect for them. Respect turned into friendship. Friendship turned into a relationship. **Remember, respect is greater than love! There is no respect-at-first sight!**

Love is a directionless destination!

The attraction is a distraction. Affection is its inception.

Typically, people believe "relationship" is synonymous with love. The person who is in a relationship has a boyfriend or girlfriend (depends on the genre), but that's not the case.

"Relationship refers to any relationship between you and that being. It might be between you and your mom or friend, you and your pet, or even you and your phone or bike. It's you and any other living or non-living being. A relationship is the bonding between two beings. It's as simple as that.

So, you have coined a relationship, but why does the relationship sound complex? Why did I face the relationship problem? Why is there some misunderstanding in the relationship? What is the root cause?

Irrespective of gender, irrespective of closeness, irrespective of your relationship, the relationship does sour sometimes. What is the reason?

So many questions are popping in our minds. It's not that easy to ignore it. It would have a huge impact on our lives. For example, if you couldn't solve this issue, you couldn't focus on work. Ultimately, you couldn't be productive. You couldn't be happy either. So, a relationship problem could affect your personal and professional life.

What is the major problem in a relationship?

One of the major reasons for a relationship is "categorizing the relationship".

Categorizing the relationship, such as whether the person is family, a close friend, or girlfriend, or a passing cloud, etc., plays a pivotal role in our lives.

You can't put every "friend" into the category of "girlfriend". But you should put your "girlfriend" into every category, like "partner," "close friend," etc. If the ball were dropped in the wrong court, you would end up getting the wrong results. Similarly, you cannot classify a "just friend" as a "close friend" or a "close friend" as a "just friend."Again, if the ball were dropped in the wrong court, you would end up getting the wrong results. We should make sure "which" person should occupy "what" category.

Just a small note: I believe I could solve others' relationship problems with my utmost experience.

How? I am an author. I have learnt so much from my past relationships. I have faced several ups and downs in my relationship. In my life, I have encountered several backstabs: bitterness, beauty, enjoyment, and care. So, I wanted to share my extensive knowledge regarding the relationship in a way that even a layman could understand.

I met a friend on a beach. He shared with me one of his life stories. He loved the girl sincerely. The girl loved him back. They would be meeting in malls and beaches regularly. The love among them was the talk of our clan.

They share each other's joy and sorrow. They help each other in finance. The girl supported his writing work; she would give him some tips and ideas as the boy wanted to be an author. The boy supported his artistic skills, as she wanted to be an artist. He would get up and leave for some location related to her art work. They surprise each other on their birthday. Our whole group was happy for them. Even each other's friends have become mutual friends for them. They seemed to be a perfect couple-made for each other.

One fine day, the girl didn't come to meet him. The guy thought she wasn't well. Some days passed, and the girl didn't turn up. He thought she was on her trip. Months passed, she didn't turn up. He wasn't sure what was going on, but he was sure something was not feeling right. On one not-a-fine-day, he received an invitation on his WhatsApp from an unknown number. He checked the invitation. He was shocked. It was from her girlfriend. It was his girlfriend's marriage but the groom was someone else.

He was absolutely upset. He had no idea in his dream that she would ditch him. She had that much affection for him and was so close to him. Days passed, his favorite hobbies waned. Drinking has been his favorite hobby for the past few days. Days passed; she was content with her husband, and he was content with his drinks. One day, one of her friends met the guy and narrated. That girl was just using him to learn how to be with a boyfriend, how to behave with a partner, how not to behave, and how to romance the partner. She just wanted to know about love, life, romance, etc., so she used my friend to find that. Some people are trying to use love for the sake of their happiness and selfishness. They need to think about the other person's feelings as well.

A relationship tip: NEVER ADJUST WITH THE PERSON YOU ARE IN A RELATIONSHIP WITH! Accept them as they are!

CHAPTER TWO

Propose: how, when, where?

Usually, people do recommend proposing in a dramatic way, or proposing by seeing through her eyes, and they usually don't recommend proposing through phones or messages. But I feel it's not how you propose, where you propose, when you propose, but who you propose that matters. If you proposed to a girl in a dramatic way, do you think the girl would straightaway say "YES?" Imagine, if a girl doesn't like a boy much, but still they both talk to each other as they were colleagues. One fine day, the boy proposes to the girl in the most dramatic way, like on a beach, arranged by event organizers, and they all stand in front of her, symbolizing "I LOVE YOU." It represents the boy proposing to the girl by using the tool as an event organizer. Do you think the girl would say "yes" to the guy? Of course not. She doesn't like the person, even if the person is rich, or well-built, or has a lavish lifestyle doesn't matter. Because the girl doesn't like the guy much. So, here, even the dramatic proposal fails. Sometimes, the most liked guy by the girl accepts the proposals even the guy proposes through phone. (Generally, proposing through phone and text is not highly recommended.) We miss their reaction to how they feel when we propose. Sometimes they say no, but their eyes and body language will tell you the truth. **Remember, it's the person who proposes to them that matters the most**. At the same time, the proposal should come from a flow. The greater the flow, the stronger the connection with your future partner. We cannot prepare a script, makes arrangements for the same, and make a proposal. Just look into your partner's eyes and propose through their eyes first. That's the key. If you lock her/him with your eye-to-eye looks, then there are more chances of getting "yes" provided she likes you. Of course, greeting cards, bouquets, and candlelight dinners still work out. But locking your eyes with her holds the top spot. Also, look into the location you are choosing for the proposal. The ambience could also trigger some kind of soft corner towards you. At least that location shouldn't be near a high traffic, noisy, sluggish location, but rather it can be cool, breezy, and feel like a good location.

It's simple:

Confidence + Ambience + Eye contact + Any gifts = Proposal

I remember one of my friends proposed by phone and got a green signal (not immediately, of course, but didn't get rejected). At the same time, I got to know a person who proposed and got rejected. So the person's contact with the partner comes into play.

The thing about the proposal is that most of the girls would never say "yes" straightaway. If the girl talks to you even after your proposal (without any "yes" or "no"), then she likes you, but she is under investigation. They will make us wait. Make the guys wait to see whether he is worth it to them. They would verify whether you were the most eligible bachelor. They would even cross-check secretly whether you have any other relationships or not. Sometimes, she would casually talk to some of your mutual friends, getting to know you from their perspective. Considering all this, we have a chance of getting a positive reply.

P.S: This is applicable to the majority of the girls. Minority and exception cases aren't considered here.

When it comes to proposals, it's simple. If you like her and want to be with her, propose to her. It's as simple as that. But remember, if she rejects you, sometimes you could lose the friendship as well. But if she accepts, you could get a friend in the form of a girlfriend. A cat on the wall kind of situation is the perfect example of this. Mostly, girls would say, "I'm not sure how I could respond to this." A girlfriend is a kind of interviewer who says, "We will get back to you in a polished way." But you have to wait for their response more than you wait for an interviewer's. Patience is the key. A proposal is a kind of test match. Trying to propose takes some time and waiting for the response gets even more time. The latter is the better.

If we are on an outing with our girlfriend, usually the guys are the ones who take their purse out. This is a general statement seen in the films. But, in reality, we should make our girlfriends pay for the bills sometimes. We shouldn't pay the bill every time. Some girls would take their purses out and immediately pay the bill. Kudos to them for those girls. They are rare. Never overlook them. But there are girls who never ever open their purses, even for Gpay or Phonepay or any pay. So for them, we should insist on paying for the bills. Money doesn't flower in the trees, and the guys aren't plucking from it. Every dollar is hard-earned money. Not everyone is richy-rich here. Companies don't offer us pay based on our gender, bills don't arrive based on our gender, so why should guys pay their bills every time? See, I didn't mean the girls who pay the bills, even though their boyfriend suggests not to. I didn't mention them. It's to the girls, who say guys are to be paid the bills. Bills are not for men. It's for the service. So, girls have to pay the bills sometimes. Splitting the bill is not highly recommended, as it would appear that we are just friends. So, if we eat in a restaurant for a day, then for the next outing, make the girl pay for the bill. That's the way it should be. And in the future, we could avoid a breakup just because of this piece of paper.

Also, try to avoid expensive gifts or expensive things for future misunderstandings. Sometimes, if a boyfriend or girlfriend buys an expensive gift for their birthday, then the other partner has to purchase an expensive gift for the other partner's birthday. This leads to continued expensive gifts.

In fact, a true loyal girlfriend expects our time, not money. The more you spend time with her, the greater the gift will be.

Also, for the birthday treat, promotion treat, or anything special, please give her a special treat. Take her out to a dining restaurant and have

Tip: Make an activity or theme park as a gift for your girlfriend's birthday; it will be remembered forever and will be cherished for all her future birthdays.

Couples find it tough to meet, or to have conversation, or to go on a date, or even to make love. It is better to have a meeting in a natural setting such as a beach, park, or any other scenic beauty. Those places could make you feel comfortable since we have already visited those kinds of places since childhood and we could be able to make a great bond in those natural scenarios rather than in a café or in a theatre. While watching children's plays, while watching the herbs or sunsets, we could be able to have some easy-going conversations and that could lead to a strong bond. The other beauty in parks or beaches is that we don't need any lavish attire or makeup, we just need to be dressed casually, like shorts and t-shirts for boys and casual tops with leggings for girls. Simplicity would bring us further close, as we don't overvalue ourselves or overdo things. So, keeping it simple and meeting in a natural place is a good way to go in the initial years of love.

If you want to know more about your boyfriend or girlfriend, take her to test cricket for at least 2-3 days. Test cricket not only tests the batters or bowlers, but it also tests the audience. It will make the audience have patience, concentration, and have interactions with their family members or friends. So, if you haven't done that, take your girlfriend to a test match and enjoy it with her. If you don't know much about your 9-5 job's girlfriend, then take her out to the 9-5 of test cricket. You would know more about her than you know her in the office. It is one of the highly underrated spots for dating. It is unique but definitely a must-try one. You could know about your patience and determination and her patience and determination. What if she doesn't like cricket? Some people would raise this question. She will come to watch the test if she loves you, regardless of whether she likes the game or not. We could have a nice lazy conversation with her and we could spend some quality time in the stadium. If your girlfriend loves cricket, then congrats, you are a lucky charm.

CHAPTER THREE

How to treat her?

We shouldn't treat our girlfriend like we are treating her as a queen, a housewife, or a girlfriend. We should treat them as though we were treating ourselves. If we treat ourselves well, then we should treat them well as well. If we don't treat ourselves well, we should learn how to treat ourselves well before treating others well. Love is not about saying "I love you" a million times. You have to show it. The action should say "I love you" more than the words. **Action is mightier than words. If we treat her like how we treat ourselves, she will treat her like how she treats herself.**

Never abuse her. We should never abuse her in any way, including cursing her, injuring her physically, such as slapping or pinching her. We should never ever abuse her. If you keep on abusing her, she will never reveal to you that she doesn't like this abuse. But she will notice everything. Abusing her like a phone battery would keep on diminishing. Even if you didn't notice her diminishing attitude, one day she will be off. And if you scream, beg, or whatever, the product won't return it to you. So, *abusing her is like a kind of suicidal bomb.* If you abuse her, you are breaking up with her. Also, we shouldn't be emotionally or mentally torturing her, like some kind of saying to her that she has no friends or family support, she should rely on us completely for everything. Even though tormenting her emotionally is not recommended, you may be the only person supporting her. But if you keep on saying this, she would believe you and she would rely on her own rather than a person who keeps on stating that she relies on him. It would be like a pin being frequently pinched on the wounded area. So, we should be aware of that as well. This is one of the most important aspects where we tend to lose ourselves.

The efforts she has made have to be appreciated sincerely, from the bottom of our hearts. She would make a good impression on us and would share anything with us, even if she was a novice in that particular field. Let's have a hands-on case study: if your girlfriend has written a novel of 40K words, you have to appreciate it sincerely. First you have to buy the book and show it to her that you have alrcady taken the first step. Even if you are not a great fan of books, you have to read your girlfriend's book. You can say that you have read her book even though you haven't touched it since you purchased it. But still, reading could make her feel like her boyfriend is very supportive. Even after marriage, her boyfriend could support her at anytime. So, once you purchase her book, read the book, and make the points you enjoyed reading, give her true, honest feedback. If your girlfriend is a graphic designer or artist, she might be able to sketch a figure well. We have to encourage her by appreciating her sketches and explaining in detail why you like her sketches. Not just saying, "It's good, it's best, or bla bla bla" or other blushing terms. We could go ahead and present her with all the drawing equipment necessary for her, like a drawing table, sketch pencils, a variety of pencils needed for drawing, etc. I don't mean to say appreciation should be expensive, but sometimes we should be in a position to afford her what she couldn't afford. It is not to impress her, but to show your love in the form of what she loves. If she loves something, you should love it too. If you love something, make her fall in love with it. Sometimes, out of our control, we would hurt her/him physically, after few days the wound in the body might get disappear but not in their mind. It would be haunting them for the next few months. Also, these hurting her through words or physical might seem like it would disappear but it won't. Like if we keep on erasing something with the help of eraser, one bad day the eraser would vanish. The same applies here, if we keep on hurting our beloved ones, our value in their life would be keep on decreasing, we couldn't find how and on what level it might decrease, but when it decreases and vanishes one bad day, then nothing remains in our life, nothing. **So never ever hurt your beloved ones. Never!**

If you had some anger on him/her, step outside of the location, make some fresh air, have some space between you both in terms of time and then step inside to the location. See, if you don't find any, just step inside the washroom, wash your face, have a hugh sigh and step into the same location. The gap and the space might help you both some tiny time to get back to normal.

Comparing our boyfriend/girlfriend with our friend's boyfriend/girlfriend is one of the worst mindsets to handle. In general, comparing is not highly recommended. Comparing one student with another, comparing one parent with another, comparing a sibling with another, is the worst culture we follow in our society. But the thing is, some comparisons won't lead us to break up. But it may lead us to the path of breakup. Sometimes, girlfriends expect boyfriends to purchase a bike. A man from a lower middle class family couldn't afford a bike. So that girlfriend shouldn't compare her boyfriend with her friend's boyfriend, because he has a bike and you don't have even a bike. And sometimes, some boyfriends might love to travel with their girlfriends. But some boyfriends don't love much travel and they love to enjoy the comfort of home. We shouldn't force our boyfriend to travel and explore things.

Sometimes, boyfriends expect girlfriends to update them on all their secrets and day-to-day activities. But some girlfriends feel shy about sharing things with their boyfriend. She won't be comfortable sharing with them. Some girlfriends might share their period dates. Some of them don't even share the day-to-day activities. So, here we shouldn't compare our girlfriend with the friend's girlfriend who shares all the high secrets of family problems. We have to understand that this is the nature of our girlfriend and the nature of our friend's girlfriend. For example, if our parent compares us with some other student, we won't break up with our parent. If a teacher compares us with another student, we don't break up with the student. If a friend compares us with some other friend, we don't break up with the friend. However, we can apply the same theory here. We can contrast our boyfriend/girlfriend with that of a friend. It won't lead you to a break-up, but it could be one of the reasons for the break-up. During a break up, your boyfriend or girlfriend might say you comparing yourself with others is one of the reasons for the break up. It will lead to a bad impression of you when compared with others. They might think you aren't that mature to handle it in a better way.

Usually, we have to understand that one person can't replicate another. Lookwise, a person might look like six others in this world. But when you look at the character, behavior, skillset, intelligence, and knowledge, one person varies from another. A person may resemble another, but they cannot share the same personality, behavior, or skill. So, a person who is an expert in coding might not be an expert in the stock market. A person who is expert in driving might not be expert in sports. A person who is an expert in teaching might not be an expert in creativity.

Watch out for her roomies? Yes, you heard it right. We have to watch out for her roomies. Her roomies influence your girlfriend. If you observe her closely, you will find so many similarities among her roommates. Most of the time, roommates can either be too close to us or too annoying to us. Even soft-innocent girls could turn into the complete opposite if you didn't track your girlfriend. There are so many girls who could influence your girlfriend in a negative way. That influence could trigger your girlfriend, and she might pounce on you. The girlfriend's pouncing on us in bed is a different ballgame, but she would pounce and fight on us during our meet ups. We were thinking about influence. What kind of influence could you please explain in detail? Right? I will explain it. For example, just as an example, the roomies of your girlfriend may influence your girlfriend to dominate you. And the roomies would be triggering it further. That's how every home functions. Husbands are dominated by their wives and have to listen to them. So, it has to be implemented right now. So, the boyfriend has to listen to the girlfriend. A girlfriend should be dominant over a boyfriend. These are the words some of the roomies might use to trigger your girlfriend. Your girlfriend might be a steady person who can analyze what's right and what's wrong. But as time passed by, these frequent words from her roomies would have a huge impact on her mind, with or without her knowledge. And if you forget to do something as simple as planning an outing with your girlfriend or something related to you both, your girlfriend will catch you and tell you that she will take over after you. Taking the ownership doesn't affect your relationship in any way, but the incidents that follow would affect your relationship. Even though she would say that both the wife and the husband can lead a happy life by giving respect and importance to others, it is not that you want to obey your girlfriend for whatever reason you say. And if you think your girlfriend started dominating even before the marriage, then the uninvited guests arrives: arguments, conflicts, and misunderstandings. You will hate her roomies. She hates your roomies. And it would result in chaos. See, it's not applicable to all the girlfriends and all her roomies or colleagues. But definitely, her roomies or colleagues could trigger your girlfriend. There might be several reasons for it, but it still could be possible because of your misunderstanding.

I remember, one of my friends told me, because of his partner's roommate, their romance was getting affected. Her roommate was getting jealous because of her romance, and her jealousy wasn't making the pair happy. So she shifted her room away from her roommate, and later, the pair was having some happy days. Even in another case, in the guys' roomies and girls' roomies, they were triggering bad suggestions. For example, in the guys' roommate, they said to control the girl and not to spend too much money on shopping; and in the girls' roommate, the girls' gang said not to travel often with friends (boys and girls) and the thing is, both those love-making parrots took the advice from their roommates and tried to control their partner, resulting in some unwanted arguments between the pair. So it's better to stay away from these negative energy people.

The more you stay with these kinds of negative people, the more you will get negative suggestions and the more likely you will fight with them.

Generally, misunderstanding occurs when we talk about others (like her friends, roommates, your friends, roomies, boss, work colleagues, etc.) rather than our own lives. Also, it's not that her roomies are to blame. The reason is that she could spend some time with them other than you or her parents. Her closest friends are her roommates. Even her colleagues aren't to be missed out. They would judge us as though we were experts in face-reading or mind-reading. If any of her colleagues or roomies commented on us regarding anything like our physical appearance, voice, job or family status, our girlfriend would act like an army and would defend us easily against them. But still, deep inside her heart, it would make her think. It would trigger it later during our casual conversation or anything. So, like tracking your expenses, tracking your girlfriend's actions and mindset, observing her closely, listening to her, you will know what lies ahead. So, if you want to unite with your girlfriend in the future, first pray that her roommates will be of nice character. *Your relationship will be smooth only if her roommates have nice character and don't influence her.*

If you are not in a position to help her, we should try to help her. For example, if your girlfriend asks you for some money for an emergency, even if you don't have the right bank balance to share it with your girlfriend, we should try to approach our friends or family and get the money from them and share it with your girlfriend. If you don't have the money, you shouldn't say you don't have it and close the connection. It would also be the end of the connection between you and your girlfriend as well.

At the same time, we shouldn't make our friends or family members share the money directly with your girlfriend, as that would lead to something else in the future. In later stages, if you don't have the money, your girlfriend might approach the person who has lent you the money directly. So, that person might take advantage and start a secret connection with your girlfriend. In that sense, he might try to flirt with her. If your girlfriend is innocent, then you won't be able to catch that backstabber.

So, simply put, you should be the intermediary between your girlfriend and your lending friend. The lending friend might be your friend, your sister, your brother, or anyone. However, make certain that this formula is followed.

If your girlfriend asks you for help, and if you aren't in a position to help her, please seek help from someone (x) and with that x support, you help your girlfriend.

Even if a step is skipped, your relationship could be in a spot of headlight. **Never avoid helping your girlfriend even if you are a ocean away from her.**

You should be a hero to your girlfriend. You can make space for your girlfriend. You can give freedom. You should be allowed to talk to anyone, any male or any female, or anyone. Making them restricted would not lead to a pleasant situation between you both. She might feel like a parrot sitting inside the cage. As the parrot wants to fly someday, your girlfriend might think the same, wanting to fly outside of the cage built by you.

At the same time, if a friend of you or her or your mutual friend tries to flirt with your girlfriend, then you know what needs to be done. But it should be done in a smooth, mature way. You shouldn't just tell her to not talk to him blindly. Tell him the reason why you're not talking to him.

For example, if your girlfriend is an artist or works as a graphic designer, and she loves sketching and painting. If her colleague or some male college mate has bought her an expensive sketch pencil, paint, brush, and an art board for her birthday or on the day of her relieving, that means that bloody rascal is trying his net to capture your girlfriend by throwing his dice. If your girlfriend has accepted his gifts, then it is a hint for him to propose to your girlfriend. If she doesn't accept his gifts, then we know she is rejecting him at the ground level. But if she accepts his gifts, then comes the irritating triangular love story. It doesn't mean that your girlfriend loves him, but it means your girlfriend loves the art gifts. But that guy might misinterpret that. So our duty is to ensure nothing goes out of her hand. We should be in a position to clearly explain how some guys could take advantage of the opportunity of presenting such gifts and trying to impress girls. We should advise them not to accept such lavish and costly gifts. Impressive and expressive gifts are a deadly combo. We should think twice before accepting it. Also, it is recommended to accept gifts made by a group of members rather than gifts presented by an individual. The people around us could take that in the wrong way, and it would be a hint for the gift presenter. They would imagine it as a green signal. Of course, we can't be with her in all the situations. But our mindset and guidance should be with her in all situations. So, by explaining things clearly, we could maintain our relationship in a smooth way.

It should be handling a kite. *Never be Hitler nor Buddha in a relationship.*

Shall we change our character for our girlfriend/boyfriend? It depends on the situation. We can completely transform ourselves because our girlfriend asked us to.

After all, she loves how we are. But at the same time, if your girlfriend wants you to change something, of course we should be in a mindset to change ourselves. For example, if our walk is not good in the sense that we walk like leaning before, then we definitely should change ourselves if our girlfriend has asked us to. And if we are too foodie and eat non-veg on a regular basis, and our girlfriend wants us to change, we can abandon these styles. We should even leave some bad habits such as smoking, drinking, etc. if our girlfriend wants us to do so. But at the same time, we shouldn't leave blindly if our girlfriend wants us to do so. We have to think whether her suggestion is worth considering. If it's not worth it, we can tell her clearly in a polished way, stating we couldn't leave that.

If we want to reject or avoid your girlfriend's suggestion, tell her when she is in a good mood. Atleast give her some chocolates or ice cream and reject her suggestion. It would avoid further arguments.

If she wants us to leave your close buddies, roomies, or any other guys or girls without any reason, never do that blindly. Ask the reason. Ask her what is troubling her to remove the contacts and then we can act accordingly. If she has a valid reason or suggestion, then it is worth considering after thinking twice. Remember, your friend is as important as your girlfriend.

Understanding the girl's psychology is simple. If she remembers your details, she likes you. Say you were born on a date of 3, so whatever the number that is offered in front of you, like choose the best number from 1–10, or any other related to that, you choose No. 3 without any hesitation. The number could be anything; it could be a lucky number, a Whatsapp forward text, or anything else, and you choose number 3 for everything. All this was noticed by your crush, and at some point, if she enquires why you were choosing number 3 all the time, then your crush has a crush on you. She notices you. Observing us is the first step toward making us feel at ease with you. That noticed thing should be converted into the next step. This notice to us is like a phone enquiry regarding joining a course. To enroll, we need to take things forward. The same applies here. Remember, we aren't trying to attract her purposely. We like her, and we are converting her into a finished product.

The next step is to talk to her directly. Never flirt with her during the conversation. Just be you. "You" are what draws her in. So, just talk how you usually talk and just behave how you normally behave. Here, we are creating a comfort zone for her. If she had a comfort zone, she would talk as she was. She would behave just like she does naturally.

CHAPTER FOUR

Personalized gifts

The topic is not completely relatable to the "How to avoid Break Up with Your Girlfriend" series, but still, this is one of the topics that should be covered under "Love subjects". This could make the bonding of couples even stronger. Gifts play a pivotal role in our love lives. Gifts should be based on money or a costlier gift. It should be the type of personalized gift that they can relate to on a daily basis. More than that, it should be touching. Touch their hearts and make them feel like you are the whole world to them. The gifts could create a sort of image for them.

Gifts always makes us connected with our loved ones. If we are keeping gifts given by our loved ones in our room, we would feel like they are with us 24*7. During the time of misunderstanding, the gifts given by them will always make them why they have started loving us. So, never underestimate gifts!

For example, if we buy some gifts, like a costly dress or a casual shoe, that's normal. And everyone around her, such as her family, friends, and colleagues, would give similar kinds of gifts. There should be some kind of uniqueness to your gift. If your girlfriend presents all the gifts on her birthday, your gift should be an odd-man-out. Being the odd man out means the gift is a unique experience for your girlfriend. And having a special feeling for our girlfriend would make us even more special. Presenting a gift that is not very relatable to her doesn't lead to a break up. But still, this could catch her eye in the gift section.

You can argue that presenting a dress, shoe, or handbag would connect with them on a day-to-day basis, and it could be touching as well. But the thing is, those gifts could be presented by anyone and everyone. And your girlfriend won't get much excitement. Though she says she is excited about the gift, in her heart she hasn't been excited.

So, what is the best gift to be presented? The response would be "Personalized gifts". Personalized gifts could have a huge impact on your girlfriend or boyfriend. It may feel like a dramatic moment, but deep down, it could have a larger impact on your partner and make them feel like you are their world and you love them so much that you won't leave them.

For example, presenting them with a greeting card that has pictures of you both, right from the first selfie to the most recent picture, consolidating them in an album.

Or presenting a video of "Happy Birthday" by your girlfriend's friends and family could have a huge impact. Of course, you can do that, edit those videos, consolidate them, and present them in front of your girlfriend, but once again, it is a little dramatic. But they will still love it, which is what is most important. *Even presenting "King-Queen" T-shirts or mugs would have a huge impact on them.* Those are the gifts that only you could present to your girlfriend. None of them could enter your world of territory. She would reveal to all her friends and colleagues that you had bought this gift for her and would say anything like the consolidated photos, video, or King Queen T shirt. Especially when she shares her happiness with her friends in front of you, the amount of happiness you feel can't match the crores of rupees.

If your girlfriend casually mentions that she wants to buy this thing, then you can buy it as well. Or sometimes, your girlfriend might say to you, "She needs to buy something like an art stand with painting brushes and sketches worth 10K rupees." She might not have bought it because she was in a financial bind. So, you can gift her that art work stand with painting brushes and pencils. That would make her feel like she had gotten a blessed boyfriend. She would never leave you, since she might have realized you were giving importance to her. If you give importance to her, you will receive importance. If you receive importance, you will be happy, as she is. The bonding gets closer and the happiness gets bigger and brighter. A simple gift could turn the table upside down. Though your love life wasn't going well, you could present her with a personalized gift, and that gift might be the one she was looking for, and as I said, the rest is history.

Never underestimate the power of a personalized gift. Also, keep an eye on the people or friends who gift her some personalized gifts. They might be dangerous in the future. Make a note of what the purpose of presenting a personalized gift is. What might their motto be?

A gift is not something given as a present to the birthday bees. It's more than that; it's a way of sharing our love with our beloved ones. Like we have seen in "Restricted Access", the gifts are like that; there is admission for everyone in the restaurant, but there isn't admission for everyone in the kitchen. In a similar fashion, there is admission for everyone who could gift our girlfriend/boyfriend, but there is no admission for everyone for a personalized touching gift to our girlfriend/boyfriend.

Not every day is special. The day our love blossoms is the most special day in our love life. How can we figure it out that that was the most special day in our lives? *It's simple: if we never check the time while on the phone or in chat, it's love.* And that call or chat wouldn't be just for a few minutes or an hour. It would be endless. We would never know what time we were crossing at. And we want even more time to spend with our loved ones. This is applicable to the time spent in person. We never want the day to end. We pray to God to stop the clock at that moment. The chat, call, or conversation would never be boring, and like water rising from the earth, we would find some topics to discuss. And both of them would want this conversation to extend to the end.

Did you ever wonder what the root cause of this beautiful time is? It would be anything like your girlfriend or boyfriend feeling lonely, or depressed, or maybe a break up from their previous love. She may even be fighting back tears for anything her professors or leaders may have yelled at her. During those tough times, she may feel alone and wants to share it with anyone who offers help.

CHAPTER FIVE

The dark side of love

Usually, people believe love is full of fun, enjoyment, romance, hugs, kisses, and various other things. This is the fancy side of love. But this fancy love is not only the process of love, and it's not always what lovers do, but it's also about pain, misunderstanding, fights, ego, possessiveness, etc. They are part and parcel of the love process. You cannot have a strong bond in love unless you face the above-mentioned side of love. They are the dark side of love. Without knowing this stuff, some people fall prey to love. That's fancy, and they are projecting the fancy side of love, which is just a quarter of the love. There are more things to be considered in the phase of love. So, never fall in love purposely for the sake of love. If you like a boy or girl and think that the person could make your life happy and you want that person to be your life partner, then you can, of course, love them.

We aren't sure when we will have romance, when we will have a kiss, and when we will fight with our partner. Even after 8 years of love, we might need to face fights and misunderstandings, but at the same time, after 8 months of love, we might have hugs and other comforts. It's about the phase, mood, understanding, and also the couple's similarities in their mindset would come into play.

There are several topics about love and marriage in our society. If you are getting married, your life is over. If you are getting married, you can't even change the channels. If you are in love, then you cannot spend time with friends. If you are in love, it is a pain- These statements are absolutely rubbish. Love makes life colorful. If you love someone, you will find a purpose in life. A clarity in life!

Sometimes, we would be with our partner and their presence would make us feel exhausted. Facing the same face, same voice, same character, same behavior, and same taste would make us a little bored of them. **We just need a break. an tiny temporary break from our partner.** Sometimes we need to stay away from them. That tiny break could solve most of the problems between us. That could make each other to think about the partner's perspective and our own mistake. It's not applicable to all. At the same time, it's not at all wrong to stay away from our partner. If things weren't going on the right track, if we felt we weren't valued, then our absence might make a reasonable difference in their mindset. So, staying away from your partner physically is one of the options to be considered. This is, of course, a temporary away from them. They say it may be 4-5 days away from them. Those days would give our partner some time to think and would realize the importance of our presence. At the same time, never use our partner's break to our advantage. Staying away from them and taking a break is like saying we need to talk to our partner through the phone or any other mode of communication, but at the same time we shouldn't speak to them like before; since we are in search of something. The tiny drawback is that we should take some breaks, but not quite often as it would become a habit sometimes. So we should take a break once in a while.

To be honest, our parents play a pivotal role in our love life. It could either be a breakup or a make-up. They have their own share of roles to play. They are the invited guests in our love life.

We should not base our decisions on those of our parents. If we were to reveal our love, the first thing about our parents would be a serious shock reaction. They never believed you would have fallen in love. We have to keep reminding ourselves that we are in love, but in an indirect way. We should update them ourselves directly with words. When we receive a call, we should avoid speaking in public. Rather, we should rush to the upstairs and speak there for more than an hour. And we should laugh at our phone, though there were repeated boring forward messages. These are the signs that we are still in a healthy love life. And would remind your parents about your love. At the same time, you should never reveal her name directly. Only direct signs could work out for parents. When it's direct, some parents could hate our partner straight away without having spoken to her even a single word. As the days pass by, they will get accustomed to it. Their minds would be settled. So, if you are in love, it is advisable to reveal your love much before the time you think of marrying. Imagine you are planning to marry at 27 or 28. Then you should reveal your love life at 25, because only then your parents could get some time to settle down and say OK. Initially, they oppose it, not because they hate love or because of caste or some other reason, but they don't realise you would fall in love. We are all children to our parents, regardless of age.So they can't take that you were young to fall in love and your love might be due to infatuation and age. So, they opposed it initially. That's the time we need to update them that our decision is correct by proving it in their personal and professional lives. Show them your professional life with the results. A good hike, a high-paying job, or a promotion could make your parents believe in you that you are not only in love but keen on professional things as well. Trust me, in India, you are considered an eligible citizen only if you own a car and a house—a status icon for our parents. For groom hunting, these play a major role. Even with our parents' permission, this car and house could make a little impact that we are responsible at the same time we are in love. *Remember, love and responsibility are different from our perspective as parents.* We also have to manage our personal lives.

Achievement in professional life can be seen in the wallet or bank balance. **But personal life achievement can be seen through our behavior.** The way you behave defines your personal life. If you talk to someone in a friendly way, build strong relationships, help others, keep your mind and body fit, etc.

It may seem a bit off-topic, but trust me, our parents note all the details. They observe us. So, these factors could come into the picture. And you can tell them that your girlfriend or boyfriend is the reason for this lifestyle. Our parents would be pleased. They will believe their child is in good hands. So, if anything, our parents appreciate, we have to tell them that it's because of our life partner. Time and again, updating our love life is important. Sometimes in an indirect way and sometimes in a direct way. The indirect way is through the phone and WhatsApp. The most direct way is through our appreciation and behavior. As simple as that, and if it is followed for more than 2 years, then we can definitely convince our parents and marry our loved ones.

CHAPTER SIX

The marriage negotiations

Definitely, if one of the partners crosses the age threshold of 25, especially the girl, then the topic of marriage comes into the picture. Some may believe that this topic is unrelated to the previous ones, but trust me when I say that it could be the cause of your breakup. So never underestimate this topic.

Your girlfriend might ask you to marry her ASAP. She wants to be secured. She wants you to reveal your love life to your parents, and she wants you to marry her with both of their parents' permission. The girlfriend would push you to get married sooner. Never go wrong with this thought. It is highly appreciated. But where the problem comes is that the boyfriend might not be ready to get married. He doesn't want a marriage any sooner. He wants to continue the bachelor life. This would be the thought of the majority of bachelors. The reason is that they don't want commitments in the early years. If they have time, they may be able to explore things before marriage, and they could risk anything in life before marriage. As they don't have any commitments, bonding, or even any sort of pressure in their lives, they just hit the office, earn money, have a romance with their girlfriend, spend some time with their friends and party, etc. So, the guys want a delayed marriage and the girls want an early marriage. Neither of those things is wrong. It's their opinions and views. But the thing is, some couples could break up and go separate ways because of these marriage topics. Though both of them are in deep love and want to marry each other, they have separate views and separate opinions.

The secret to marriage is that there is no age limit for marriage. There is an "age" in the term "marriage", but there is no age for getting married. We can get married at 25, we can get married at 30, and we can even get married at 35. **The only question we have to ask ourselves is, "Are we ready for marriage?"** If we are prepared, we can go for it; if we are not prepared, we can postpone it. There is nothing wrong with that. But make sure you aren't married too early or too late.

How can we differentiate "Are we ready" from "not"? If we are mentally, physically, financially, and emotionally prepared for ourselves, then it is time for us to tie the knot. But financial readiness could be achieved even after the marriage. As a result, financial matters may be postponed. But the other things, mental and physical, should be ready, and even in terms of psychology, we have to be ready.

How could we know that we are ready? What are the factors we can consider that we are set to save the date?

First, we should have enough life lesson. It's called experience, not in terms of work, but in life experience. Only life experience could lead you to a happy marriage. When to react, when to argue, when not to react. When to argue, when to compromise, when to zip the mouth, when to unzip the mouth. We need to know all this. We should have faced and experienced all this in our lives. We should know and act according to the situation. That's when we can marry. It's not a "to do list" or something "DIY" kind of thing. But it is highly recommended to have life experience before the bells ring.

Even a breakup could lead to a happy marriage life. We would be depressed after the breakup. We don't connect with anyone. We are all alone. But in due course of time, we have to get married. At one point, your parents would push you to get married. And at that time, after the marriage, your life could be blossoming as you have had the experience of "how not to break up with your girlfriend." **As a result, the experience will assist you in leading a happy marriage life.**

At the same time, girls should understand that marriage is not about age. We shouldn't force the guys to get married soon. The guys need some time to settle down and finish some personal tasks like getting their older brother or sister married. or even starting a start-up. or even further education. Or even going abroad. So they could do all sorts of things. If you put too much pressure on the guys, they may become irritated, and the romantic conversations between you will be strained. Leave the romantic talk to us. The general day-to-day life would be hell. So, understanding the guys is important.

Also, guys should understand the girl's situation. We could convince the girls, not the girls' parents. We can persuade the parents that "marriage is not about age." Though we can say that marriage is not based on age, in small towns and villages, marriage is based solely on age. If they are 25, they should get married so things can be sorted out. That's what's happening in India. Also, God has created the most beautiful creatures on the planet in the form of relatives. They could be working as a backend for your marriage. Screw the Java, PHP, and Python-relatives are the best backend tools for you, especially when it comes to marriage. The girls couldn't handle the pressure created by the family. The guys don't know the pressure being created on the girl's family. Being a girl in this society is tough. The more they try to avoid the marriage, the more pressure it creates for them. They couldn't avoid it. Like a surprise party, some of the relatives threw a surprise groom-seeing session for the bride. Balancing the office work, family pressure, and the boyfriend's delay, it all adds up to a catalyst for the girls to hate the boyfriend's life. The guys have to understand from the girl's perspective. So, understanding girls is crucial.

At the same time, guys don't know what's happening in girls' lives. So it's the duty of girls to explain things clearly. The guys couldn't understand it. They have their own problems. As a result, it is preferable for girls to share things that bother them and for guys to share things that bother them. Only sharing their stress could solve the problems. Since you share, the less you share, the more likely it is that your relationship will end. You didn't provide enough details to your partner. So explain things without hate, shouting, and irritation. *All good things come to couples who share their problems and seek the best solution for them.*

CHAPTER SEVEN

Breakup series: How to resolve the fight with your girlfriend?

First of all, fighting is a process in a relationship. We can't skip the fights and misunderstandings. If we try to skip the small fights, like trying to avoid the small fights or arguments, then one day all the gathered small fights will bulge up and burst open. All our inside-out feelings and opinions would fire up against our girlfriend, and she would enquire about hiding these feelings, and there would be the breakup. For example, if a guy is close to your girlfriend, say he is your girlfriend's bestie, but you don't feel comfortable with his presence or his friendship with her, Then ask your girlfriend about that bestie; seek out an answer then and there. Never keep these opinions or feelings in your heart. If you want to ask, just ask. Only keeping inside would lead to the fighting, not because of asking. Of course, once you ask, she will fight with you, but that little fight could change the topic easily and we can bring the situation back to normal. Imagine there was a huge argument between you and your girlfriend. When you tried to change the topic, you couldn't. It would be too late, and even if you tried to switch the topic, the old topic of argument would come into the picture. So, if you want to argue, please argue at that moment. If you want to fight, please fight at that moment. After all, she is your girlfriend.

The catch is that fighting and arguing should be kept as a secret sauce. We shouldn't use it too often, but we shouldn't use it at all. If you used it too often, the relationship would become bitter and your girlfriend wouldn't feel happy being with you. And, if you didn't use it, you wouldn't have a smoother relationship. She would take you lightly. As I said before, it should be like handling a kite.

For example, if you are waiting in a park for your girlfriend and she arrives late to meet you, then you shouldn't pounce on her and start an argument with her. That's not necessary. You can just troll her and leave her alone.

During the conversation, you came to know that she went to meet her school/college/office friend during the weekend without your knowledge. You should have pounced on her at that moment.

You have to know when to argue and when not to argue; that defines who you are. That would keep your love life balanced. *You will be in trouble if you argue for the "not-to-argue-things" while not arguing for the "argument-things."Clarity is necessary for us.*

Another major issue that causes misunderstandings is not giving enough private space to our girlfriend or boyfriend. We should understand that everyone needs some private spaces for things like doing things that they love. It may be anything from watching movies, reading books, travelling, playing cricket etc. It may be anything, but we should understand that we cannot be with our partner all the time. We will each have some time to ourselves. And we need to spend some time with our family and friends. We have heard of "work-life" balance, but we should also have "love-life" balance. It may sound unique or even awkward to some, but it's a deep statement. As much as we spend our time with our partners, we should spend some time on ourselves. That would give you the pleasure of spending time with our partner. We can devote all of our time to our girlfriend or boyfriend. That may work out for the initial years of love, but as years pass by, we will come to know the power of "love-life" balance. So, even if your girlfriend/boyfriend couldn't understand this theory, make them clarify the point. We should be in a position to explain things in the way they love us without being harsh.

For example, your girlfriend is asking you to take her out on the coming weekend. But there is an ODI match between India and Pakistan on Sunday. Imagine you are a die-hard cricket fan. Of course, you are a die-hard fan of your girlfriend, but at the same time, you are a die-hard cricket fan. So, you say that there is a cricket match on Sunday and you cannot take her out. She doesn't accept your reason and says you have to take her out or else she won't speak with you for some days. Again, you try to convince her, but she is adamant. She is not happy with you. And she believes you are not giving importance to her. Here, how you handle this situation is what defines you. At this moment, we shouldn't shout at her or create any kind of scene. You have to explain to her clearly that you give importance to her. And she is your first priority, always. But, we can't see the India-Pakistan match quite often, and you tell her that this is important at that moment. It is not important to her, but only on that Sunday is it important.

Say that you can meet her on any day, but that the match cannot be missed, and state the importance of that. And you promise that you will take her out the next weekend. Never forget to praise her, as any such kind of previous encounter would have happened and your girlfriend could have left you to do as per your wish. Mention that incident. Make her feel important and that importance would say "yes" to watching the match. And never think that you are getting permission from her. It's not permission; it's emphasizing information over permission. As some of them would say, "So, you are not asking permission, you are giving information." So at that time, say, "It is not information, it's importance." Rather than saying, "Why should I ask your permission?" Or do you try to control me? " Also, please don't suggest to wash her clothes or meet her friends at that time. She would have planned something and she would say, "I know what to do." You should please watch the match, "like smashing the door on your face." And you would be angry at her. Argument 2.0 begins once more. So, leave it as it is. This is not applicable to the boyfriend handling the girlfriend. This is vice versa as well, and it's applicable for girlfriends handling boyfriends. Don't become an "argument boyfriend" or an "argument girlfriend".

During these argumentative times, think twice before you talk.

Most couples believe that once they get married, they have had success in their personal lives and have achieved things they wanted. But the real catch is that the battle only begins right there. Marriage is not the end, it's the beginning. In fact, the loved couples didn't want to marry; they wanted to lead a happy life. So they must marry in order to live a happy life. Marrying our loved one is a process, not a destination. The real process is staying with our loved ones and making them happy. By seeing them happy, we would be happy.

Also, the crucial part is that, whether it is a love marriage or an arranged marriage, we need to start things from scratch. Couples during love won't be the same as couples after marriage. Things change, and responsibility emerges. We can't be relaxed and funny all the time. The real difference between a love marriage and an arranged marriage is that we know our partner's fault. That's a love marriage. We don't know how our partner arranged the marriage.

So whatever the marriage could be, however close you could be, whatever the profession you do, it doesn't matter. All you need to know at the end of the day is to start over and love again. After marriage, you have to repeat all the things you have done during your love life. You have to buy some gifts for your girlfriend/boyfriend, take her out for dinner, surprise her by taking her to the theme parks, and most importantly, you have to care for and love her as you have loved before. The love should be missed. It can be increased but shouldn't be decreased.

CHAPTER EIGHT

What if the misunderstanding happens again and again?

This is another sensitive topic. Also, this depends on the perspective. Most of them would agree with that. Some of them would ask questions about it. Anyhow, this is not just a topic for the relationship, but this is a serious junction in their personal lives. What if a misunderstanding happens again and again in our relationship? How should I solve this tough nut? I have solved a misunderstanding recently, and again, there comes another misunderstanding with our beloved ones. This is happening frequently, more frequently than an Android update version nor a Corona update version. What should I do now? Should I try to resolve the problem or should I end this call forever?

Ending a relationship is easy. But the time you spent, the love you gave, the affection you had, the efforts you made, the care you had, the care you got, would be completely shattered. That should not be our mindset. In the worst-case scenario, even if you split up with your partner, you will have to start over. So just ignore this.

The first misunderstanding comes from miscommunication. Communication should be clear between you and your partner. For better communication, you should be transparent in each and every aspect.

Sit with her. Speak with her. Spend time with her. Make her comfort and be open.

We have to make her comfortable. We can only make her comfortable if we have better communication with her. So you have to find some space, like parks or beaches, to hang out and pour your heart out.

Make her feel that they are the most important thing in your life. Everything else is secondary. Make sure your inner feelings tie a knot with their inner feelings. Before you start leaving that place, she/he should realize that you are their entire world. It should be dramatic, but it should also be unique and come from the heart. Only then, it would take several days for the next misunderstanding. Otherwise, it would keep coming back.

Frequent misunderstandings come from serious uneasiness on your part. There was some expectation from your partner which you failed miserably, which led to a scar on your partner's mind. That in return, she can't control her emotions and fights with you frequently.

You have to ask what her expectations were. She would be reluctant at first, but in the course of time, she would convey her expectations and what you lacked in those. Listen to her. Never interrupt or argue with her in between. Interrupting or arguing would never lead to solving the misunderstanding. Make a mental note of all the points you were about to make. And never pounce on her with your points once she has completed her point. First, I appreciate her for sharing all the details. This would be professional, but appreciative in the way you want to appreciate it. It can be anything romantic. Then speak out on the points that you have on your side. Never defend for everything and never accept for everything, even if you have every reason in the world to defend yourself.

Check with your partner whether you can compensate for that expectation right now. If you can do so, she will be glad and the pain that carried her for so long wouldn't be on her mind. Make sure you aren't just doing that for the sake of it, but from the bottom of your heart.

If you couldn't do that at that moment, apologize to her and promise her you won't repeat the mistake again (even though you have said this a million times). You want to make her smile in that meeting. That should be your motto.

Shall we hunt for a girl or a boy? The heading looks obscure. But this is one of the underrated topics to be discussed. Some people, repeating again, would be searching for a girl or a boy to love. Like a fisherman, he uses a net to hunt the fish in bulk. We cannot do that in love. We shouldn't be in the mindset of hunting girls or boys for love. We cannot do that. Love should happen. We cannot chase love. Love should chase us. If you are in the process of chasing girls or boys for love, then trust me, you aren't going to find true love. Love should occur without our intention. Like purchasing many lottery tickets and expecting either one of them to get clicked for a lottery ticket, we cannot expect to love many girls or boys, of which one will turn into your girlfriend. That would be a non-sense idea. This is love, not a lottery.

We will not fight with some anonymous people in real life. People have a tendency to fight with their closest friends. If we aren't fighting with some friends, then they might not be in our close circle. We would only show our faces with our closed circle.

When our partner fights with us, it means they adore us. They want us to be a better person; they want us to be safe; they want us to have a good heart; and they want us to be a better partner!

But in some cases, our partner might not be in the right state to accept the fight. Some fights are like passing clouds; they come, they rule us, they make us think why we are in a relationship, and they leave. They are just like us day in and day out. We can neglect that. But we should never neglect the root cause of the fight. The root cause is what our partner is expecting from our end. How can we try to make our partner happy by resolving the root cause of the issue? If we can do that, then the fight will be resolved. Also, the partner who is fighting with us should not be too harsh in terms of words or action. Sometimes, people would remember the harshness but not the reason for the harshness. So try to be a cool-headed person when we are fighting, at least not a hot-headed person.

Marriage is a single-day event, but marriage life is not an event, it's a process. So choose your partner wisely. He/she might be of our taste, may not be of similar taste, may be similar in things, may not be similar in things, but at the end of the day, you both should have a strong understanding. The understanding should be deep-rooted and even though you fight for several things in your head and mouth, you should be united in heart.

Separated by mouth, united by heart.

Trust the process and go with the flow. Sometimes, we wonder whether our choice is perfect, whether our love life will continue the same even after marriage, or whether we need to reconsider the situation. So many factors would be running in our minds. But believing in your love outweighs everything else.

You can be an ultra rich person, you can be one of the most successful sports people, you can be a great investor. You don't even have a stable job. Your startup would be ruined. You might be uneducated. It doesn't matter when it comes to love.

People say love is blind. It's not only about looks, it's about the qualifications, job, bank balance, caste community etc. Only love can defeat all this crap.

This is the most common problem people have. They would share their personal relationship problems with their friends. Most of the friends would try to sort out the problem, but that's where the real problem arrives. The friends would help the couples to sort out their problems, but it was just a temporary problem that they had solved. The real issue is that the couple has shared their close personal relationship problems with their friends. So their friends get to know their problems, which is highly dangerous. **No person in this world should know the problems of a couple, including their parents** (unless or until it's a topic to be discussed, which is exceptional). Couples should never indulge in their personal space to expand and share it with others. Even though the couple was in some misunderstanding, even though the couple didn't speak to them for some weeks, even in the worst case, the couple had broken up, they shouldn't be in a position to share their problem with anyone.

Another major blunder is that couples tend to share their secrets with their friends. Sometimes this would happen when the couple was in some misunderstanding, and by mistake, one of the partners could tend to share the other partner's personal secret with any one of their friends in a fit of anger or frustration. That personal secret could reach your friend circle if you have mutual friends. In that case, the problem might disappear, but this sharing of the partner's secret tends to make friends or mutual friends, which might be the real problem for the couple. So, never ever share the partner's secret or your problem with the partner with anyone. It might be a friend/well-wisher/parents/siblings. We should never reveal it.

CHAPTER NINE

Why does the breakup happen?

Or even during these COVID times, due to long distance relationships, so many relationships have turned into Titanic ships. Some of them have sunk. because long-distance relationships are difficult for couples to manage. Long-distance relationships are never easy. We can work from home, we can connect with an NRI friend through a video, we can gain knowledge from the internet, but we can't love our loved ones through long distance relationships with the help of the internet, insta, or whatsapp. They are the tools for communication. You're the communicator.

Also, we should be in touch with her often. For example, x (boy) and y (girl) are college lovers. They were studying at the same college and love blossomed for them. If the boy and the girl go apart in terms of their work location or higher studies, they might not spend some quality time as before during their undergrad. They might feel some distance in their relationship or one of them might feel insecure in their relationship. One of them might wonder whether this relationship would last long. Irrespective of how close you are you might feel the insecurity. You might wonder whether this love lasts (this is applicable only for the long-distance relationship), so we should be in touch with them quite often. X, the boy should visit her during her birthday, new year, or any other special day. It's in the hand of the boyfriend to be in touch with them. The boyfriend should gift her whatever she loves on that day. It is recommended if the boyfriend takes her out to a nearby theme park, amusement centre, or activity centre. This is better than taking her to cinema theatres, or malls, or some standstill places. We should take her to activity-centered places, so that the day could be memorable and that day would stay with her for some months, until his next visit. *Remember, the girls are just like the kids. If you know that, you know that!* Of course, in this internet world, we could stay in touch with our mobiles or whatsapp. But staying in touch with them in person is what matters the most. The more you spend time with her, the more she loves you. It's as simple as that.

The reason for the break up should also be taken into consideration. Of course, I don't justify the breakup, but it depends on the reason for the breakup. I will categorise the break-ups as "valid break-ups" and "invalid break-ups." Valid breakups are allowed in real life. The break up is not a harsh call. The broken-up person is not a harsh person. **The situation might have made the partner break up. But their love might have been true.**

For example, if the boyfriend is abusing or involved in domestic violence with his girlfriend, then the girlfriend has all the rights in the world to break up with her boyfriend. The reason for this breakup is valid. But her love would have been true.

At the same time, if the girlfriend breaks up with her boyfriend just because the latter earns less pay when compared to most people, If she is breaking up with her boyfriend because her family doesn't like him, then the reason for this break up is invalid. Her love was not true.

So, only the reason for the break up could determine whether the break up is OK or not. **Not all breakups are good. Not all break-ups are bad.** Sometimes, the situation could push you into something where you don't have any other option than to break up with your partner.

I will show you yet another reason for a valid break up. Another major reason for breaking up is that the love shown in the initial years would be drastically reduced. In the initial years of their love both the boy friend and the girlfriend would be in deep love, because they were new couples. But when the new couple gets old, when this couple has been involved in love for nearly 4+ years, then there comes the challenging phase. The boyfriend or girlfriend might get bored of the partner; they might know the real face of the partner. For example, the girlfriend thinks the boy was super cool, happy to roam, heroic, easy-going, so in the initial phase, the boyfriend would be such and the girlfriend's friend felt comfortable with that. But as the days passed by, the girlfriend might have gotten tired of his character. He might not be too interesting to him. He might be a little less heroic, innocent, not a brave and bold man. So, the girlfriend's love might have gone down. See, in the initial phase of love, we know the positive side of the person, but when we love a person for more than 3 or 4+ years, we tend to know the negative side of a person. At least not a negative side, we could call it a person's weak side.A person who is joyful and friendly to the outside world may be sad and depressed inside. A person who is shy and reserved for the outside world could be crazy inside. So, to get to know the person completely, we need a few years to get to know him.

If we draw a graph, stating the girlfriend's love, then it might be kind of an "L" shape, where her love was at its peak at the initial phase and, as time passed by, her love was reduced and it went low. She won't agree with him, she won't respond to him properly, and she won't show any interest whatsoever, when she believes, whatever the boyfriend says, he must be wrong, just because he was innocent. He must be cool and easy to roam, but at the same time, he could be innocent and less intelligent with less bravery. So, there comes the misunderstanding. Never allow a misunderstanding to come between you. It will slowly eat you, love, and burp you with ego. So, it has eaten the girlfriend's love and burped her ego. So, she has never admitted or moved in with the boyfriend. And so, because of this hectic pressure inside him, he wants to break up with her. So, that break up is valid.

Relationship tip: During phone communication, never end the conversation with anger. Your anger will kill your relationship one day.

CHAPTER TEN

How to handle the break-up!

Obviously, this is a diametrically opposed topic to the title of this book, but to be practical, we can be certain that all the love that turns into family. Yes, breakups happen. The boy could break up the girl. The girl could break up the boy. Or it might be a mutual break up, whatever break up could be on the cards. In fact, facing a breakup is the most common thing in love compared to turning it into a family.

Anyway, coming back to the topic, how to handle the break up?

It is one of the toughest situations one could ever face. You can face anything; you can face being unemployed, dropping out, a failed startup, or even being fired from a company, but you cannot face a breakup. It's hard to handle.

The sole reason is that when you are started to love, we would consider that love as a token of marriage. We never think of the other ways of getting broken up. When we think of the most positive people in this world, we would imagine convincing our parents, getting married to our loved one, having kids, building our dream house, living with our parents, having our dream car. So we would be imagining or even be in a fantasy world. So we never think of any negative state: what if our love didn't succeed; what if we break up; what if we stop loving after marriage; what if our parents don't support our love; etc. So, the couple lives in a fantasy world. To be honest, nothing is wrong with this. If being positive is a fantasy, of course, you can be a fantasy. But, sometimes, out of our control, out of our grip, the situation changes.

Suddenly, all the fantasies we have built would start thrashing one against the other. Either the boyfriend started hating the girlfriend or the girlfriend started hating the boyfriend, or their parents were trying to break their love, or a third person could come into the picture in between the couple, etc. These may be the kinds of situations a couple could find themselves in during their fantasy love time.

A break is not a COVID-19 condition or a general feeling of unease. If you face a breakup, it's not a condition, it's a lifestyle. Since we would be sharing all of our details, secrets, and day-to-day activities with them beginning on the day of love. For our girlfriend/boyfriend, we would be involved in some special things, like dropping her off at her hostel daily, buying her the favourite Kitkat chocolate from the department store, having a date at the regular restaurant, or hitting the regular park or beach you used to go to. So it's high time for us to change our lifestyle. It is highly recommended to avoid visiting these places where you have spent the most time. The more you visit these places, the more memories you will gain. Also, the most important thing is, the more you try to avoid her memories, the more memories your mind will fetch. The biggest database in the world is our mind. It would fetch the unwanted data at the unwanted time. So, never mess with the mind. It's not that we shouldn't think of our ex, rather we shouldn't think **"We shouldn't think of our ex"**. The point is, we shouldn't try to erase the memories of your ex. Leave it as it is. If you have memories related to your ex, keep them. If you face your ex in your dream, face it. Those 100s and 1000s of moments can't be erased instantly. We don't have those options on our mind. So, just live with those memories. At some point in time, we will forget it without our consciousness. Those, of course, could hurt you until your last breath. But that's the way life is. We have to face it, we have to heal, and we have to go back to basics.

Typically, your breakup period defines your personality. In the initial days after breaking up, you don't notice much difference, and you don't miss your ex-girlfriend either. The days would be normal, like any other day, and you would have the impression that you weren't speaking with your ex-girlfriend because she was on a tour or something. But when the days pass into months, after nearly 6 months of breakup, comes the really challenging phase. You will miss your ex-girlfriend badly. You are incapable of handling the situation. All her memories would come into the picture. She would haunt you in your dreams. You can't get with other people quickly. You will smile, but you won't be happy. You would eat, but only for your stomach. You will talk to people, but you won't get attached to people quickly. You would talk to girls but maintain a distance. You would try to avoid romantic movies. You'd watch the lip lock scenes, but your thoughts would wander to the lip lock you had with your ex-girlfriend. At least once a day, you will remember her. You wished to wish her happy birthday. You will visit the places where you have visited with your ex-girlfriend. Even a crore is not a compensation for the beautiful, priceless time you spent with your girlfriend.

Those were the days, long gone. Previously, you would be sharing your stories with your girlfriend about your friends. After the breakup, you will be sharing your stories with your friends about your ex-girlfriend. Time changes; life changes; people change; situations change.

If you can handle a breakup, you can handle anything in life. Being jobless is a different kind of pain. I don't want that to be compared with this pain. But breaking up is a different kind of pain that can't be expressed. You can get a job at any time, any day, and you can recover from the jobless situation. However, this can be applied to the breakup situation. This means you can't love another girl to forget your ex-girlfriend. That's not highly possible. Love cannot be conditioned. If that's a condition, that's not love.

There are two types of people in this world after a break-up.

First, just after their breakup, they would commit to another love, another girlfriend or boyfriend, another life.

Second: Thinking of their ex and spoiling their current and future lives by drinking a lot, smoking, drugs, etc., spoiling their skills, talent, health, wealth, family, friends, and finally spoiling themselves entirely. That's the second type.

Second, it is not at all a mature way to handle the breakup. Few people think they could smoke, drink, and use drugs to forget their ex. In fact, these things could trigger your emotions and make us dream about your past life. Also, there is no happiness that lies in smoking or drinking. Only your health is spoiled. The drink is mixed with alcohol and not mixed with any other substance, like "drink to forget your ex." These are just kind of cinematic things. Never ever try that path.

The first one, obviously, I'm not a great fan of loving another girl just after their breakup. But sometimes that is the way it is. But if it happens accidentally and you fall in love with another girl within a matter of months, that is fine. But some people will purposely fall in love after their first breakup. If you purposely fall in love, you didn't fall- you failed. You can purposefully fall in love. Love is not a whatsapp status to showcase yourself. Love is our salary, in fact, like a period of days. It's a secret. It is not to be shown to everyone. That's not the best way to live a life. If updating the girlfriend is cool for some, then they don't understand what love is.

CHAPTER ELEVEN

What should we do after breaking up?

See, something isn't in our hands. We couldn't be 100% sure our love would succeed. It's out of our reach. We can love completely, but we cannot be certain that our love will result in a love marriage.

Facing the breakup is hell. The thoughts will haunt you forever. Breaking up is like a ghost. It will haunt you forever. You can get away from it. This ghost acts quite uniquely. If you love truly, it will haunt you daily.

We can forget about our girlfriend/boyfriend. But we can't forget the memories created by our girlfriends or boyfriends. The memories will kill us. In particular, we would have fixed our minds that our love would unite and turn into a marriage, but things would take a drastic turn and life would start to change and it would result in an unfortunate breakup.

First, we should delete her/his contacts. That is most important. The more the contact gets saved on the phone, the more you tend to text or call him or her again. So delete it. Before deleting, block the contact and delete it. The reason is that though we delete the contact from the phone, we can't delete the number from our memory. That's hard to erase. We might save the number again in the future. So, block the contact and delete it.

Clear all the photos and videos involving her. If you have any of her/his photos, erase them. Also, the videos should be wiped out completely. Not to forget, the photo or video taken by her has to be removed. The reason for this is that if you see the photo again, the memories will flood back into your mind, and her memory will haunt you once more. You can restart your life. So, not only to remove all her pics or videos, but also to remove all pics and videos taken by her.

Clear out all the chats and call history. All our call history would be dominated by our girlfriend or boyfriend. Like Aussies dominating the 2000s era, our phone would be dominated by her calls and texts. So it's clear The reason is that sometimes we would want the old message to be re-read and realize how beautiful life was. The time would have passed, the naughty romance, silly fights, would have been pictured in front of you. Some tears would be shed from our eyes. Our lives would want those beautiful moments back with her. So, never keep the chats and call history. Remove them entirely. Even the WhatsApp call, Zoom call, or whatever the call you have had, erase it. Likewise, the emails.

Reset the password for all our social media accounts. One way or the other, we would have shared our social media credentials with our ex-dear ones. Definitely, they won't miss-use the credentials. But on the safer side, try to change the password for our social media. Never forget to reset the password for social media.

Also, block her/him on all social media. If not, one not-a-fine-day, we would search for her profile on Facebook or Instagram and we would be staring at their pics. It is advisable to block her/him on all social media. so that their visibility shouldn't be seen anywhere.

Some of our friends might urge you to speak to them and try to unite with them. Never allow such things. Once a glass is broken, it is broken completely. I didn't say that a broken up couple shouldn't reunite. Of course, they can. But that's not a TV remote to turn on and off. Before breaking up, the couples should decide whether they have to break up or they have to unite. If they want to break up, they can go ahead and break up. If they have to unite, then, of course, they can go ahead and reunite. Everything depends on the couple's decision. But the thing is, both of them should think of the same thing. If either one of them is not satisfied with reuniting, then the plan should be dropped. On the other hand, if either one of them is ready to break up, then the plan should go ahead and break up. Because we can live a happy life with an unhappy partncr. Mark it out.

Never ask your mutual friend about him or her. Generally, it is not advisable to ask about his/her life updates. may not be in a direct way. If we come to know that they have moved on and they have got another partner, then that's hard to accept. So, you'd better stay away from the updates of your ex. "Live and let live". This should be the mantra for all broken up couples.

More than anything, never ever try to disturb them in any other way. If they want happiness without your presence, leave them. Never try to stock them with the help of your friends or mutual friends; that's not the right way to approach the break up. Also, never try to create a fake account on social media and try to be in contact with them. Though you could approach them in an indirect way, the misunderstanding between you doesn't fade away. After all, it's not the account that matters, it's the perspective and the behavior that vary. So, it could seem you can win her back after the breakup with some fake accounts, but at the end of the day, that won't be the outcome.

We couldn't answer this question simply by saying "Yes" or "No." It depends on a lot of situations. Of course, we can reconnect with your ex-girlfriend or boy friend, but remember why you left her/him. If you have a valid answer to this question, go ahead and rejoin your girlfriend and start loving again. But the thing is, your partner should feel the same way about rejoining you; otherwise, there is no point in rejoining.

Sometimes, rejoining would be the best decision and sometimes avoiding the rejoining would be the best decision. All it can be said by your love and the reason for the breakup. There is nothing wrong in either of the choices, but you shouldn't regret for the decision, that's the key. Regretting of rejoining could kill you inside if the comeback relationship didn't go as per your plan.

Sometimes, staying away from the girlfriend and quietly praying for them is the best solution for any breakup. Allow them to live their lives while you live yours. Not to disturb each other post-breakup.

The real character of a person could be determined by a man with a broken heart. A man or woman with a broken heart is like a new born baby, a clay pot, or even like water. It depends on how we shape ourselves. We can smoke, drink, and spoil ourselves, or even take this as a challenge, take this situation as a motivation, and come up in life. At the same time, even though we come up in life, a break is a break up. A broken heart is a broken heart and can be reattached. But it will heal in the course of time. A new love could blossom, a new life could emerge, a new purpose could be formed, anything could happen in life. So staying positive and determined and focusing on the work is important.

Of course, it is easy to say. However, we have control over the pain. We can handle that rage. The result of our partner is unthinkable. Even in dreams, we would never think of a breakup. But it has happened in reality. So we would have the pain and anger. But take that anger on a positive note.

I will state that with a real-life case study: in a cricket match, there was some dispute between a batter and a bowler. The bowler appeared to have incited the batter to fight. The batter has just arrived at the crease and has faced nearly 6 balls. But because of the bowler's attitude, the batter got angry. He didn't pull the bowler's collar and roll up on the pitch. Rather, he owed it to himself that the bowler should apologize to him. In the next over, for the next 6 balls, the ball went flying and it cleared all the balls over the boundary line. That incident happened in the 2007 T20 World Cup. That bowler is Flintoff, and the batter is Yuvraj Singh. Yuvraj Sign hit six sixes in the 18th over of Stuart Broad. After this was over, Flintoff came to Yuvraj and apologized for his incident. That's the thing. That's Yuvraj. Later, that match proved to be crucial for India, and India went on to win the match and the world cup. But that 18th over was a turning point for India in that world cup. And that's how we should convert our pain and anger into something special.

The Final Philosophy

All we need is to be in a good relationship with a true partner. At the same time, we must consider whether we are true partners to our partners. We have to answer it from the bottom of our hearts and be true to ourselves. While asking ourselves, if we find it "yes," then it's cool. If "no," then we need to think about why we aren't true. We need to think about that.

www.ingramcontent.com/pod-product-compliance
Lightning Source LLC
Chambersburg PA
CBHW061359160726
47995CB00001B/386